JOHN WHITE

FUNNY CHRISTMAS STORIES TO READ ALOUD

No part of the contents of this book may be reproduced or transmitted in any form or by any means without the written permission of the publisher.

Table of Contents

Like father, like son 4

Santa Claus Meeting 5

The reply of a child 6

The sky is congested 7

The meaning of Christmas 8

A desire granted 9

Gifts for stockings 10

Misheard lyrics 11

Misunderstood in translation 12

Honesty is the best policy 13

The Christmas Loser 14

Methods To Predict a Cold Winter 15

Two Stupid Reactions to Cold Weather 16

Did You Know? 17

Seat Yarn in the Stand 18

Try Before You Buy! 19

Mirror Image 20

At Christmas, an Amusing and True Funny Story 21

The Traditional Christmas Pudding's Story 22

An Amusing Christmas Turkey Story 23

The Christmas Queue Idiocy 24

A Short Funny Xmas Story 25

Christmas Hold-up Tale 26

A Nice Drink 27

Grandpa's Story 28

Like father, like son

When I got home from work one evening, the lights were turned out. My wife had prepared a beautiful candlelit meal, and our two young sons, Garett and Seldon, were dressed to the nines.

"Hey, didn't we pay our hydro bill?" I joked.

"Hey, Dad, did they not pay their hydro bill, too?" Garett inquired a few months later during the Christmas Eve illuminated procession, when the church was crowded and silent.

Santa Claus Meeting

My husband accompanied our two sons, Devin and Chase to a celebration where Santa would be handing out presents. The organizers requested that we bring our own gifts, so I brought beach towels with the children's names written on them.

Devin couldn't believe the skinny Santa was actually Santa when he arrived. When he unwrapped his present, his skepticism gave way to belief.

He said, "He has to be the real Santa!" "How would he know my name any other way?"

The reply of a child

Our annual trips to the local Christmas tree farm are some of my favorite childhood memories. My children may still participate in the ritual by accompanying my parents when they cut down their tree, even if we have an artificial tree at home.

When I told Ethan, my six-year-old, that we'd be helping them pick a tree the following weekend, I expected him to be excited.

Instead, he questioned, confused, "What did they do with the one we gave them last year?" with a worried brow.

The sky is congested.

My four-year-old son, Max, was staring intently out the airplane window on a ride to Mexico for Christmas vacation. We'd just taken off and were flying into a thicket of large white clouds. Max appeared to be worried, and I wondered what he was thinking about.

His eyes widened and a broad smile spread across his face. "Mom!" he exclaimed loudly. We're caught in all this snow, which is why we can't get anyplace!"

The meaning of Christmas

For children, figuring out how Santa fits into the religious significance of Christmas can be difficult. My two-year-old daughter, Josie, demonstrated this by pretending to read from a book: "Then Santa forgave them their crimes..."

A desire granted

My mother is a bit of a hoarder. She discovered a birthday card I had sent her 30 years ago while digging beneath her stairs for some Christmas decorations. She called to tell me that my desire for her had been granted.

"What wish do you have?" I inquired.

"You wished me a happy 30th birthday and hoped I'd live another 30 years—and I did!" Mom answered.

Gifts for stockings

My husband put a variety of cosmetic goods in my stocking one Christmas. When my eight-year-old son, Callum, strolled in, I was going to wash off one of the facial masks. I told him it was a gift from his father and that it would make me attractive.

As I cleaned and rubbed my face dry, he patiently waited by my side.

"So, what are your thoughts?" I inquired.

"Oh, Mom, it didn't work!" . Callum was the one who responded.

Misheard lyrics

My niece's class of six-year-olds sang "Hark, the Herald Angels Sing" at a Christmas show when she was in school. For this age group, the statement "God and sinners reconciled" was a challenge.

"God and sinners dressed in style!" exclaimed one tiny boy, whose voice completely drowned out the rest of the chorus.

Misunderstood in translation

My children and I stopped at a tiny store on our way home from visiting family over the holidays. "Was Santa good to you?" the clerk asked my four-year-old daughter.

"Her name isn't Tia," my five-year-old son said, not used to the Ottawa Valley accent.

Honesty is the best policy

Gabriel, my nine-year-old son, had learned at school that Santa wasn't real. "Dad, tell me the truth," he said as he approached me. "Does Santa exist?"

I made the decision to inform him that we were the ones who had purchased his most recent Nintendo Wii game.

"Are you serious?" he asked. "It would have been better if you had let Santa bring it." It would have been free that way."

The Christmas Loser

After returning home late from a night out, a young man attempted to enter his house by the chimney. He didn't want to wake up other residents at the Judson Center social services agency; he'd also broken his curfew and didn't want to get into any trouble. He ascended onto the roof and down the chimney in full Santa Claus regalia; however, he was too huge and became stuck. The 17-year-old began moaning, and his cries were heard and he was rescued. He had to be rescued by fire fighters and police officers from the city of Royal Oak, Michigan, in the United States. The youth suffered from minor scrapes and bruises.

Methods To Predict a Cold Winter

A Native American tribe's chief was questioned by his tribal elders in early September whether the winter of 2011/12 would be cold or mild. The chief inquired of his medicine man, but he, too, had lost touch with the natural environment around the Great Lakes in terms of reading signs. In reality, neither of them knew how to forecast the impending winter. The chief, on the other hand, chose a more modern method and dialed the National Weather Service in Gaylord, Michigan. The meteorological officer informed the chief, 'Yes, it is going to be a cold winter.' As a result, he returned to his tribe and instructed the men to gather as much firewood as they could. The chief called the Weather Service a fortnight later to inquire about the situation. He inquired, "Are you still predicting a cold winter?" The weather officer said, 'Yes, it's extremely chilly.' Following this brief discussion, the chief returned to his tribe and instructed his people to gather all of the wood they could locate. The chief called the National Weather Service again a month later, this time to inquire about the upcoming winter. 'Yes, it will be one of the coldest winters in history,' he was told. The CEO questioned, 'How can you be so sure?' 'Because the Great Lakes Native Americans are collecting wood like crazy,' the weatherman explained.

Two Stupid Reactions to Cold Weather

1) This is a true story about John Porter, a resident of New York State in the United States, whose home's pipes froze one winter. Mr Porter backed his car up to an open window, hoping that the exhaust might warm up the home and help them unfreeze. a two-gallon container of gasoline, heated Porter, his wife, and their three children were brought to the hospital with carbon monoxide poisoning a short time later.

2) George Gibbs of Columbus, Ohio, was burned in the second degree on his head. This is how it went down one bitterly frigid winter morning. George identified his car's inability to start as a frozen fuel line, which he felt he could fix by pumping warm gasoline through it. He then attempted to heat a two-gallon can of gasoline on his kitchen gas stove.

Did You Know?

The recent cold wave that has caused havoc in parts of the UK also has a lighter side. 'The Open Air Winter Wonderland Show in Cardiff, Wales, has been closed due to the snow,' according to a BBC Radio notice.

Seat Yarn in the Stand

Freddie and John had a season ticket to Chelsea and were able to watch the team play. They couldn't help but notice that there was always a spare seat next to them (B14), and they had a buddy who would be interested in purchasing a season ticket if they could all sit together. Freddie went to the ticket office one halftime and inquired if they could buy a season ticket for B14. Unfortunately, the official stated that the ticket had been sold. Despite this, the seat remained vacant week after week. Then, much to Freddie and Eddie's surprise, the seat was taken for the first time that season on Boxing Day. 'Where have you been all season,' John couldn't help questioning the newcomer. He replied don't ask; the wife had purchased the season ticket last summer and saved it as a surprise Christmas present.

Try Before You Buy!

Myra needed a new party dress for her office's Christmas celebration. 'May I try on that dress in the window, please?' she said in the clothing store. The salesgirl replied, 'Certainly not, madam; you'll have to use the fitting room like everyone else.'

Mirror Image

Nathan thought it would be great to get his wife a small gift for the next day on Christmas Eve. He was always short on cash, so he pondered what that present might be.' Unable to make up his mind, Nathan went into Debenhams and asked the girl in the cosmetics section, 'How about some perfume?' She displayed a £75 bottle to him. [$150USD] Nathan grumbled, 'Too pricey.' For £50, the young lady returned with a smaller bottle. 'Oh gosh, there's still far too much,' Nathan grumbled. The sales girl, irritated by Nathan's rudeness, pulled out a miniature £10 bottle and presented it to him. Nathan grew upset to the point of rage. 'What I mean is, I'd want to see something incredibly cheap,' he grumbled. As a result, the saleswoman handed him a mirror.

At Christmas, an Amusing and True Funny Story

Authorities have informed Will and Guy that a seven-year-old child was stopped by police in northern Germany while attempting to shovel snow with a front loader borrowed from his parents' business. After clearing the street in Reinfeld and heading back to the parking area, officers on patrol discovered the boy atop the 3.5-meter-tall [11.5-foot-tall] excavator. When the child noticed the police car approaching him, he instantly came to a complete stop. 'He unlocked the door, stepped out, and instantly stated that he didn't have a driver's license,' according to the police report. When asked why he started plowing, he stated it was because his father was upset about the quality of the roads. He got in his car after seeing the key in the ignition. The key to the loader was recovered from the toddler and returned to his mother, along with the boy.

The Traditional Christmas Pudding's Story

Martha decided to keep up with the times and give microwave cooking a try. Her faithful husband Archie responded by purchasing a brand new top-of-the-line Sharp Microwave oven for her. As Christmas neared, Martha gathered the ingredients for her Christmas pudding recipe. She continued in the conventional manner, even having each family member stir the mixture 'for luck.' When Martha looked up the cooking time for a classic Christmas pudding in the microwave's handbook, she couldn't believe it was just ten minutes. As a result, she opted to cut down on her usual cooking time of 50 minutes. Martha was engrossed in her favorite television show in the living room and did not notice the pudding spitting in the microwave oven, nor did she hear the mini-explosions. After nearly an hour on 'High,' she finally removed the pudding from the microwave, which smelled like burnt sugar and looked like a ball of tar. The Christmas pudding, predictably, was a disaster, so bad that Martha couldn't even probe it with a fork. In fact, the black ball became lodged at the bottom of the bowl, and Archie had to pry it out with a screwdriver. Martha flung the shriveled Christmas pudding to Togo, her St Bernard puppy, in a fit of rage. She saw the funny side after a few days, and Togo adored his new unbreakable toy, which kept him entertained until the next Christmas.

An Amusing Christmas Turkey Story

Sarah, the young new bride, cries out to her mother. 'Richard doesn't appreciate what I do for him,' she sobs. 'Now, now,' her mother reassured her, 'I'm sure it was simply a misunderstanding.' 'No, mother, you don't get it.' 'Well, the nerve of that awful cheapskate,' her mother recounts. 'I bought a frozen turkey roll and he raged and screamed at me about the price.' 'Those turkey rolls are only a few dollars,' . 'No, mum, it wasn't the turkey's price.' "Aeroplane ticket..." "What did you need an aircraft ticket for?" 'Well, mother, when I tried to mend it, the directions on the package said to "prepare from a frozen state," so I flew to Alaska.'

The Christmas Queue Idiocy

I was shopping at a toy fair in Worcester shortly before Christmas when I noticed a line at the doll stand, where people were waiting for Mattel dolls to be refilled. Looking around, I noticed a dear buddy of mine waiting in line. 'Hey, Lennie,' I exclaimed, 'I hadn't realized you collected dolls.' 'I don't,' he laughed. 'Then you must be buying a Christmas present then?' 'No, not at all, my buddy,' Lennie said, his eyes gleaming happily. 'If you don't mind my asking, Lennie, why exactly are you standing in this particular queue?' 'Oh that,' he laughed. 'It's like this, my pal, I've never been able to resist a Barbie line.'

A Short Funny Xmas Story

An upright politician, a giving lawyer, and Santa Claus all boarded the Ritz Hotel's lift (elevator) shortly before Christmas. One by one, they discovered a £50 note laying on the lift's floor as it traveled from the 5th floor to the ground level. Which one took the £50 bill and handed it in at the front desk? Of course, Santa is the only one who exists; the other two don't!

Christmas Hold-up Tale

It was Christmas Eve, and the department store manager was just paying off Father Christmas in his office. Suddenly, a youngster appeared and demanded that the manager hand over the considerable profits. The manager was at a loss for what to do, so the teenager attempted to use his gun to persuade him to open the till and hand over the money. Despite the fact that the robber pressed the trigger, nothing happened, so he peeked down the barrel and fired again. It worked this time.

A Nice Drink

Jimmy drove his van two days before Christmas to pick up a group of open jail convicts. His duty, as usual, was to transport them to a local hospital for radiation treatment. One of the 12 volunteered to buy Jimmy a drink because it was Christmas. So they went to the Rose and Crown pub and had a wonderful drink together. Jimmy took a detour to the men's room on his way out, and when he emerged from the restroom, all of the inmates were vanished. He drove about for half an hour, looking in all of the pub's bars, but there was no trace of the convicts. They'd all managed to flee. What options did Jimmy have? He made a hasty decision to stop at a particularly long bus line and inform the passengers that he was a relief bus. He then took the first 12 prisoners and drove them to the open prison. He then radioed ahead to the warders, informing them of the 'Code Yellow' situation. This was a pre-planned signal that some of the inmates were acting strangely. Jimmy quickly emptied his passengers before fleeing. Surprisingly, his deception was not revealed until after the New Year.

Grandpa's Story

Grandpa concluded that Christmas gift shopping had become too tough. He decided to send each of his grandchildren a check because they had everything they needed (check). 'Happy Christmas Grandpa,' he wrote on each card. 'Buy your own present!' says P.S. Conclusion: While Grandpa was enjoying the family gatherings, he noticed that his grandchildren seemed a little distant. It lingered in his thoughts well into the New Year. Then, one day, he was cleaning up his study and discovered a small stack of cheques (checks) for his grandchildren under a pile of magazines. He'd entirely forgotten about them when he was putting together the Christmas cards.

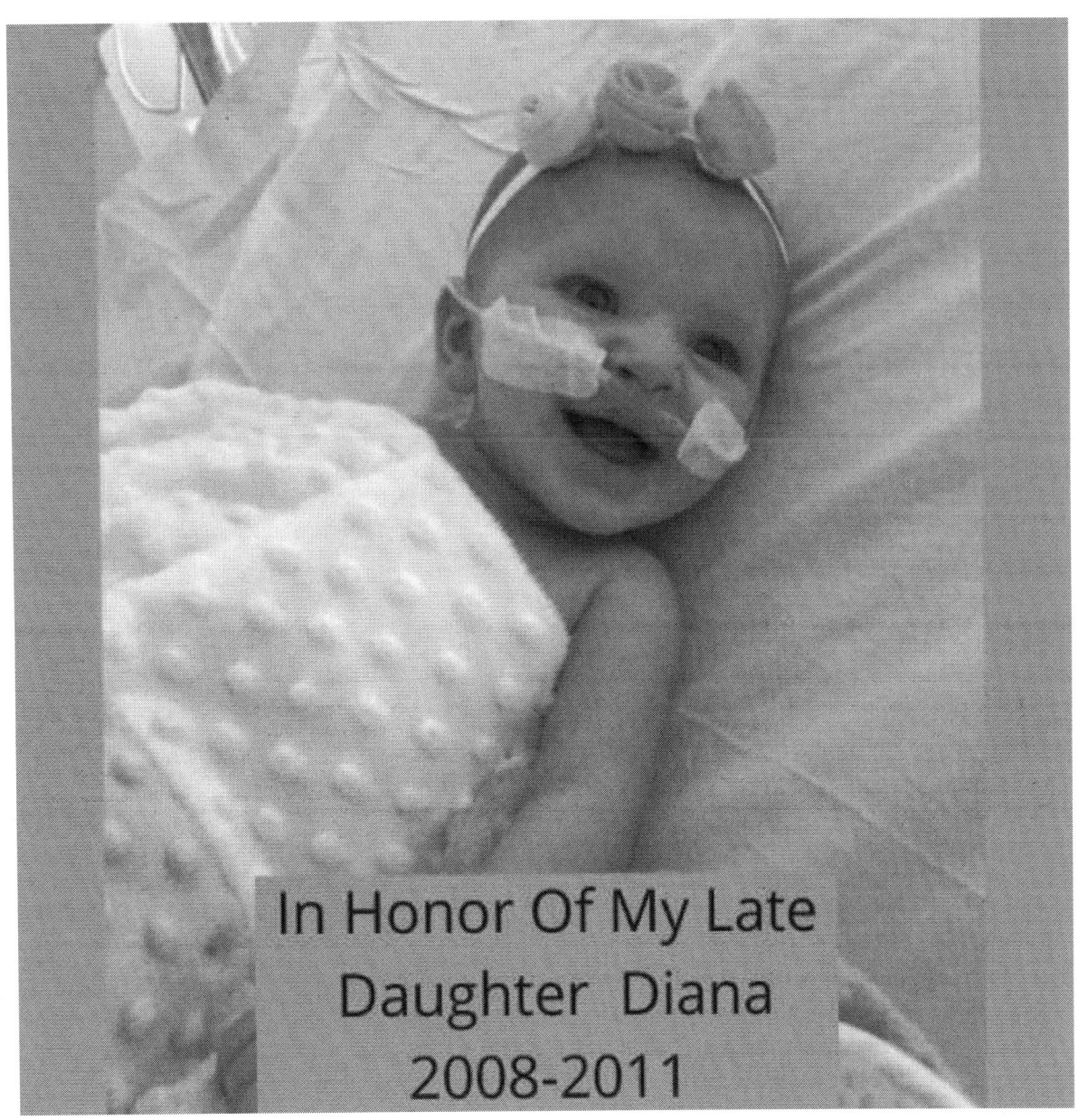

In Honor Of My Late Daughter Diana 2008-2011

Printed in Great Britain
by Amazon